**Dear Parents,**

Welcome to the Magic School Bus!

For over 20 years, teachers, parents, and children have been enchanted and inspired by Ms. Frizzle and the fabulous cast of beloved characters that make up The Magic School Bus series.

The unusual field trips, visual jokes, eye-catching details, and interesting information are just a few of the elements that make The Magic School Bus series an excellent tool to get your child excited about school, reading, and exploring their world.

It is important that children learn to read well enough to succeed in school and beyond. Here are some ideas for reading this book with your child:

- Look at the book together. Encourage your child to read the title and make a prediction about the story.
- Read the book together. Encourage your child to sound out words when appropriate. When your child struggles, you can help by providing the word.
- Encourage your child to retell the story. This is a great way to check for comprehension.

Enjoy the experience of helping your child learn to read and love to read!

Visit www.scholastic.com/magicschoolbus to subscribe to Scholastic's free parent e-newsletter, and find book lists, read-aloud tips, and learning hints for pre-readers, beginners, and older kids, too. Inspire a love of books in your child!

There are many Magic School Bus books for your reader to enjoy. We think you will enjoy these, too:

Ms. Frizzle

OUR
SOLAR
SYSTEM
SUN
MERCURY
VENUS
EARTH & MOON
MARS
ASTEROIDS
JUPITER
SATURN
URANUS
NEPTUNE
PLUTO &
KUIPER
BELT
COMET

Liz

Written by Kristin Earhart
Illustrated by Carolyn Bracken

Based on The Magic School Bus ® books
written by Joanna Cole and illustrated by Bruce Degen

The author and editor would like to thank John M. Stoke, Manager of Informational Education for the Space Telescope Science Institute's Office of Public Outreach, for his expert advice in preparing the manuscript and illustrations.

ISBN-13: 978-0-545-08602-8
ISBN-10: 0-545-08602-7

12 11 10 9 8 7 6 5 4 3 2 1          9 10 11 12 13 14/0

Designed by Rick DeMonico

First printing, January 2009
Printed in the U.S.A.

# The Magic School Bus®
## Blasts into Space

Arnold   Ralphie   Keesha   Phoebe   Carlos   Tim   Wanda   Dorothy Ann

Cartwheel
·B·O·O·K·S·®

SCHOLASTIC INC.

New York   Toronto   London   Auckland   Sydney
Mexico City   New Delhi   Hong Kong   Buenos Aires

"Let's play my space game," said Carlos.
"Great idea, Carlos," the Friz says.
"To the bus, kids!"
Liz beats us out the door. She loves trips.

I HAVE A FUNNY FEELING ABOUT THIS.

CAN'T WE JUST PLAY THE GAME HERE?

Ms. Frizzle turns the key,
and the bus lifts off!
A screen appears at the front of the bus.
"It's my game!" Carlos yells.

CLASS, WE'RE GOING TO GET A GOOD LOOK AT SPACE.

WHAT'S SO GOOD ABOUT IT?

BLAST OFF!

9

"D.A. got it right!" Carlos tells us.
"If we win, all the buttons will be green."
All at once the bus speeds up.

STAR LIGHT,
STAR BRIGHT
by Wanda

Stars are balls of gas. They make their own light.
The sun is very hot and very bright.

There are billions and billions of stars.

Many stars have planets. Our sun has eight planets.

We whiz away from the sun.
We pass two planets.
The next riddle shows up
on the screen.

RIDDLE #2:
I HAVE ICE ON THE
TOP AND BOTTOM,
AND AM RED IN
THE MIDDLE.

VENUS—SECOND PLANET
FROM THE SUN

MERCURY—FIRST PLANET
FROM THE SUN

13

The next planet is blue and green.
"It's Earth!" Wanda says.
"And there is the moon, going around it," says Phoebe.

IS "EARTH" THE ANSWER TO OUR RIDDLE?

EARTH HAS ICE ON THE TOP AND BOTTOM . . .

MOON

. . . BUT IT'S NOT RED IN THE MIDDLE.

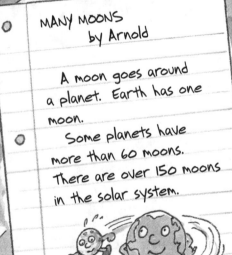

MANY MOONS
by Arnold

A moon goes around a planet. Earth has one moon.
Some planets have more than 60 moons. There are over 150 moons in the solar system.

14

"Let's keep going, class," Ms. Frizzle says.
"You will find Mars very interesting."
We watch Earth get smaller.

LOOK—MARS HAS ICE ON THE TOP AND BOTTOM!

AND THE MIDDLE IS RUSTY RED!

AND OUR BUTTON IS GREEN!

15

We hop back on the bus.
We fly deeper into space.
"Watch out!" Keesha calls.
"We almost hit that big rock!"

THOSE ARE SPACE ROCKS.

THEY ARE CALLED ASTEROIDS.

I CALL THEM SCARY.

We pass the giant asteroids.
Space is dark and cold.
We can see stars far away.
We get a new riddle.

RIDDLE #3:
I GO AROUND AND
HAVE A TAIL.

A TAIL? IS IT A SPACE DOG?

MAYBE IT'S A
SPACE LIZARD!

GET SERIOUS! WE'RE
RUNNING OUT OF TIME!

We wonder what in space has a tail.
Just then, something flashed by.
"Class, that is a comet," the Friz says.
"It goes around the sun."

IT GOES AROUND!

AND LOOK! IT HAS A TAIL!

IT'S NOT A DOG OR A LIZARD
— IT'S A COMET.

THREE RIDDLES DOWN.
TWO TO GO!

YES!
A COMET!

A COMET'S TALE
by Carlos

Comets are made of ice
and dust. That's why they
are sometimes called dirty
snowballs!
A comet's tail is made of
bits of gas and dust that
have melted off the icy ball.

SUN

COMET

Carlos looks at the clock.
"We have to hurry," he says.
"Step on it, please, Ms. Frizzle!"

HURRY,
HURRY!

We come to a GIANT planet. It looks like it has a big red eye. "That's Jupiter's great red spot," Tim tells us.

JUPITER—FIFTH PLANET FROM THE SUN

THE SPOT IS A HUGE STORM, TWICE AS BIG AS EARTH.

THE STORM HAS LASTED FOR OVER 300 YEARS.

I'D HATE TO BE CAUGHT IN THAT STORM!

Beep! Beep! Beep!
"Oh, no!" Carlos yells.
"That's the warning bell.
Our time is almost up!"

SATURN—SIXTH PLANET FROM THE SUN

BEEP!

BEEP!

BEEP!

RIDDLE #4:
I AM A RING, BUT I DON'T GO ON YOUR FINGER.
I AM A BELT, BUT I DON'T HOLD UP YOUR PANTS.
WHAT ARE WE?

BEEP!

Now we have passed all of the big planets.
We land on Pluto.
It is cold and dark.

Liz has a map!
Pluto is in the Kuiper Belt.
"Kuiper" rhymes with "wiper."
It is full of big rocks and small planets.

27

We only have one riddle to go!
We only have one minute to go!

BEEP! BEEP! BEEP! BEE! BEEP!

60 SECS

RIDDLE #5:
I'M NOT TOO CLOSE, I'M NOT TOO FAR, I'M JUST THE RIGHT DISTANCE FROM YOUR STAR.

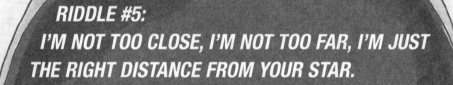

Back in our classroom, we made a model of our solar system. We were happy to be on our home planet again . . . for now.

NEPTUNE

SATURN

ASTEROID BELT

MOON

EARTH

MERCURY

SUN

LIZ'S MARS ROCKS

COMET DUST

31

# SPACE IS A GIGANTIC PLACE

The Magic School Bus is really magic.
Even the fastest rocket could not travel
from the sun to the Kuiper Belt in a day.
It would take 9 ½ years to make this trip.

| | | |
|---|---|---|
| **MERCURY**<br>[Closest planet to sun] | | **Size:** Smallest<br>**Time to orbit sun:** 88 days<br>**Moons:** None<br>**Rings:** No |
| **VENUS**<br>[2nd planet from sun] | | **Size:** 3rd Smallest<br>**Time to orbit sun:** 225 days<br>**Moons:** None<br>**Rings:** No |
| **EARTH**<br>[3rd planet from sun] | MOON | **Size:** 4th Smallest<br>**Time to orbit sun:** 365 days<br>**Moons:** 1<br>**Rings:** No<br>Has plant and animal life |
| **MARS**<br>[4th planet from sun] | DEIMOS PHOBOS | **Size:** 2nd Smallest<br>**Time to orbit sun:** 687 days<br>**Moons:** 2<br>**Rings:** No |
| **JUPITER**<br>[5th planet from sun] | | **Size:** Largest<br>**Time to orbit sun:** 12 years<br>**Moons:** At least 63<br>**Rings:** Yes |
| **SATURN**<br>[6th planet from sun] | | **Size:** 2nd Largest<br>**Time to orbit sun:** 29 years<br>**Moons:** At least 60<br>**Rings:** Yes |
| **URANUS**<br>[7th planet from sun] | | **Size:** 3rd Largest<br>**Time to orbit sun:** 84 years<br>**Moons:** At least 27<br>**Rings:** Yes |
| **NEPTUNE**<br>[8th planet from sun] | | **Size:** 4th Largest<br>**Time to orbit sun:** 165 years<br>**Moons:** At least 13<br>**Rings:** Yes |